The Election ISBN 978-0-9930773-0-2
Fisherton Press Ltd

www.fishertonpress.co.uk

First published in 2015 in the United Kingdom

Text © Eleanor Levenson 2015
Illustrations © Marek Jagucki 2015

ISBN 978-0-9930773-0-2

A CIP catalogue record for this book is available from the British Library.

The Election

Words by Eleanor Levenson

Pictures by Marek Jagucki

Published by Fisherton Press

With thanks to the many
Kickstarter funders of this book.

"There's going to be an election," said Mummy, looking up from the newspaper.

"What's an election?" Alex asked.

"Well Alex," said Mummy, "an election is when we decide who is in charge."

"There's going to be an election," said Mummy.

"Yes," said Daddy, "we should help our party."

"Are we having a party, Daddy?" Alex asked.

"No Alex, a party is the name for a group of people who are standing for election together because they believe the same things," said Daddy.

"Because they want to be in charge?" asked Alex.

"Yes," said Daddy.

"I have got us a poster," Daddy said to Mummy.

Mummy helped Daddy stick the poster to the window.

"The party we support has stripes on its posters," said Daddy.

The poster could be seen by the whole street.

"There's another poster on our street," said Mummy.

"It's for the spotty party," said Daddy.

"The spotty poster is in Evie's window," said Alex.

"Why do you have a spotty poster in your window?" Alex asked Evie, in the park.

"Because my Mummy and Daddy want the spotty party to win the election," said Evie.

"Come on Alex," said Daddy pulling on his coat. "We have work to do."

Daddy was holding a pile of stripy leaflets.

"We have to put one through every door on the street," said Daddy. "Will you help me?"

"Okay," Alex said.

"Hello Alex."

It was Evie and her Mummy.

"Hello Evie, what are you doing?" Alex asked.

Evie held up some spotty leaflets.

"We have to put one through every door," she said.

That night Alex asked Mummy a question.

"What's the difference between the stripy party and the spotty party?"

"Well," said Mummy, "they have different ideas about how they would run things if they were in charge."

"We like the stripy party because we think their ideas are better," said Daddy.

"Come on Alex," said Mummy the next day.
"We have work to do."

Mummy had a clipboard and a pen and a stripy sticker.

"We have to talk to everybody who lives on our street,"
said Mummy, "and persuade them to vote for our party."

"Hello Alex."

It was Evie and her Daddy.

"Hello Evie, what are you doing?"
said Alex.

"We have to talk to everybody on the
street," said Evie, "and persuade them
to vote for the spotty party."

One evening Mummy and Daddy wanted to watch the debate on television.

"What's a debate?" Alex asked.

"It's where the leaders of each party tell us why they want to be in charge," said Daddy.

The next day Daddy looked excited.

"Today is election day," he said.

"Let's go to the polling station and vote," said Mummy.

"What's a vote?" asked Alex.

"It's where you say who you want to be in charge," said Mummy.

"Sometimes you use a pencil to put an X in the box next to the name of the person you want to be in charge," said Daddy.

"And sometimes you mark the names in order of who you like most," said Daddy.

"And sometimes you tell a computer how you want to vote," added Mummy.

That night Mummy and Daddy put the television on.

"We will find out who has the most votes," said Daddy.

"The party with the most votes will be the party in charge," said Mummy.

"But the results will be very late and now it's time for bed," said Daddy.

The next morning Mummy and Daddy looked grumpy.

"Did the stripy party win the election?" asked Alex.

"No, the spotty party won," said Mummy.

"But I wanted the stripy party to win because we worked very hard with our leaflets and clipboard," Alex said.

"Me too," said Mummy, "but this time more people wanted the spotty party to be in charge than the stripy party."

"Maybe they won't be so bad," said Daddy.

"And maybe the stripy party will win next time," said Mummy. "Now eat your breakfast and then you can go and play with Evie."

Acknowledgements

Eleanor would like to thank all the Kickstarter funders of this project, Marek Jagucki for his fantastic illustrations and help beyond what was expected, her parents Ros and Howard for political conversation from day one, and Leo, Connie and Richard for continuing this tradition, even at the young ages of 2, 4 and 34.

Marek would like to thank Hannah and Oscar for putting up with all the late nights working; Ellie for sharing her project; all the Kickstarter funders; Rachael, Simon, Tanya and Steve at Sira Studio, Harrogate for keeping me company. The Thom Hartmann Program for making my head explode. Gem the dog for the hairy desk.

If you enjoyed this book...

Tell:

- your local librarian
- your teacher
- your friends
- your local bookshop

Write:

- to us general@fishertonpress.co.uk
- blog about it
- on social media #FishertonPress
- review it online

Buy:

- a copy for a friend
- birthday presents
- other Fisherton books
- donate a book via our website

www.fishertonpress.co.uk

Lightning Source UK Ltd.
Milton Keynes UK
UKOW07f1249300916

284197UK00001B/2/P